For Joyce Sweney,
A fantastic teacher, writer, and friend.
Big huge hugs and kisses!
—L.B.F.

For my parents
—B.P.

Honestly, Mallory!

by Laurie B. Friedman

illustrations by Barbara Pollak

Carolrhoda Books, Inc.   Minneapolis • New York

CONTENTS

A FAIRY TALE FROM MALLORY

Once upon a time, there was a princess named Mallory. She was a lovely child who always tried to do the right thing. But sometimes, doing the right thing was hard. It was particularly hard when other people did annoying things that made her, as her mother the queen seemed to like to say, "react without thinking."

The queen always told Princess Mallory: DO NOT REACT WITHOUT THINKING BECAUSE THAT IS HOW YOU GET INTO TROUBLE. But Princess Mallory didn't always follow her mother's advice. Career Day at

6

Fern Falls ... Here's what happened:

Some of the kids in Princess Mallory's class were bragging about being good at stuff. They said that for them, deciding what to be on Career Day would be a breeze.

All this talk about other people being good at things and knowing what they want to be when they grow up annoyed Princess Mallory.

Then someone (her lifelong best friend, to be exact) gave her an idea. At long last, the princess had figured out what she was going to be on Career Day.

But alas...when she got to school and said what she was going to be, something horrible happened. Some of the kids laughed at her.

This annoyed Princess Mallory even more. So, without stopping to think about what might happen, she told a little lie, and that's when her fairy tale turned into a big, fat mess.

STARS EVERYWHERE

"Rise and shine! It's Saturday!" I say to Cheeseburger.

I scoop up my cat and do a little dance with her around my room. We both love Saturdays. At least, I think we both do. I know I do. I just wish Saturdays happened more than once a week.

I pull on jeans and a T-shirt. "What do

you think we should do today?" I ask
Cheeseburger while I'm brushing my hair.

Even though Cheeseburger can't answer,
I know if she could, she would say that we
should call Joey, my next door neighbor,
because that's what we do every Saturday.

I tuck my cat under my arm and carry
her into the kitchen. I grab a doughnut
with one hand and pick up the phone with
the other and dial Joey's number.

It rings twice, then Joey picks up.

"Hey," I say when I hear his voice. "Want
to meet outside by the wish pond and we
can skateboard?"

I wait for Joey to say "sure," but that's
not what he says.

"I can't today. *Remember*, I told you I
have soccer practice?" He says *remember*
like he can't believe that's something I
could forget.

"Tell her the championships are in three weeks and the star goalie has to be in tip top form," I hear Joey's dad say in the background.

"The championships are in three weeks and . . ."

I cut Joey off before he gets to the star goalie part. "Maybe some other time," I say into the phone.

"Sure," says Joey.

I hang up and look at my class phone list that Mom tacked to the bulletin board. If Joey can't play, I will find someone who can. I dial my desk mate Pamela's number.

"May I please speak to Pamela?" I ask when her mom answers the phone.

"I'm sorry, Mallory. Pamela isn't home right now," says Mrs. Brooks. "She's at her violin lesson. Didn't she tell you that she's playing a solo at her recital next month?"

"No, she didn't," I say quietly.

"Pamela is going to be the star of the show," Mrs. Brooks says. "She's planning to invite you to come hear her play."

"That sounds great," I say and hang up the phone. But the truth is, going to hear Pamela play doesn't sound great at all. What sounds great is finding someone who wants to play today.

I look at my class list again and put my finger on Danielle's number. Even though we're in the same class, we never do anything together because Danielle is always doing things with Arielle. I can't decide if I should call her or not.

I do *eeney meeney miney mo* to help me decide. I land on *don't call,* but I do anyway.

Danielle answers. "Arielle?" she says, like she was expecting her to call.

"No," I say. "It's me, Mallory."

"Oh," says Danielle, like the sound of my voice is as disappointing as finding out you're having a pop quiz in math. "What do you want?" she asks.

It's kind of hard telling her what I want. Even before I do, I feel like I know what the answer will be. I swallow. "Do you want to come over today? We can play outside and paint our toenails."

"I can't," says Danielle, like she doesn't even have to think about her answer. "Arielle and I have dance practice. Our recital is in two weeks and we're doing a duet." ,

Danielle keeps explaining. "Arielle and I have the most important parts. I'm the sun and she's the moon. Everyone else is a star, and their job is to twinkle around us."

"Oh," I say, like I see what she's talking about, and I do. Even though Arielle and Danielle are not the stars, they really are.

I hang up. It seems like everybody I know is a star at something. I scoop up Cheeseburger and plop down on the couch in the den. "If no one wants to play, we'll just watch our favorite show," I whisper in her ear.

Cheeseburger purrs, and I click on the TV

so we can watch *Fashion Fran.*

"Now for the latest designs that sparkle and shine," says Fran. She models a top and skirt covered in sequins. "It's so shiny that if you wear this top and skirt combination outside on a sunny day, you will positively glow."

Fran smiles at the audience. "That's all for today," she says. "And don't forget that in two weeks we'll announce the winner of our *Kids Can Fashion Design Contest.* Just think . . . one lucky winner will receive an all expenses paid trip to New York and will get to model his or her custom design on a special episode of my show. I hope you all entered," she says. Fran blows a kiss and waves good-bye.

I click off the TV. "I don't know why I didn't enter that contest," I tell Cheeseburger. "I wish I had."

And I bet I know someone else who wishes she'd entered too. As official lifelong best friends, Mary Ann and I like a lot of the same things, including this TV show.

I reach for the phone to call her, but before I can get it, someone grabs it, and that someone is Max.

"Hey!" I say trying to get the phone from him. "Don't you know about *ladies first*?"

Max looks around the room like he's looking for something. "I don't see any ladies," he says. "Anyway, I have an important call to make."

"So do I," I say.

"I doubt it," says Max. He looks at the TV screen. "There's only one person you would be calling while you watch that show, and I don't think calling Birdbrain counts as an important phone call."

I can't stand it when Max calls my best friend Birdbrain. But before I can tell him how much I don't like it, he starts punching numbers into the keypad.

"Hey, Coach," he says. "What time is practice today?"

Max listens, then says "great" and hangs up. He throws the phone at me. "Here you go, now you can call Birdbrain. I've got to go to baseball practice. The All-Star playoffs are in two weeks," he says.

When Max leaves, I reach across the couch and pull Cheeseburger close to me. I rub her back. It seems like everybody I know is a star, even my brother.

I pick up the phone and slowly dial Mary Ann's number. I know my best friend will understand when I tell her how I'm feeling.

The phone rings twice, then Mary Ann answers.

"Hey, hey, hey!" I say. I start to tell Mary Ann how everybody around me is doing something special, but she starts talking before I even have a chance to say a word.

"Mallory, I can't talk," she says. "I'm on my way to the mall to do a hip hop demonstration. I'm the lead dancer, and I get to wear a tie-dyed T-shirt with sparkles all over it and a matching hat. Wish me luck," says Mary Ann.

I hear Mary Ann take a deep breath like

BASEBALL STAR

FASHION STAR

MUSIC
STAR

HIP HOP
STAR

DANCE stars

ME

she's super excited about being the lead dancer in a hip hop demonstration.

"Good luck," I say.

"Thanks," says Mary Ann. "Got to go. Got to sparkle." She laughs at her joke.

But I don't. I can just picture Mary Ann sparkling at the mall.

I can also picture Joey sparkling on the soccer field, Pamela sparkling at the violin hall, Arielle and Danielle sparkling in the dance auditorium, and Max sparkling on the baseball field. I can even picture Fran sparkling when she goes outside.

There's only one person I can't picture sparkling, and that one person is me.

ANNOUNCEMENTS

"Girls and boys, I have an announcement to make," says my teacher, Mrs. Daily.

I love when Mrs. Daily starts the week off with an announcement . . . especially when it's a good one, which I hope this one is.

"What do you think she's going to say?" my desk mate Pamela whispers to me.

"I'm not sure," I whisper back. "But I hope she announces that we don't have any homework for the rest of the week and that she brought in cupcakes to celebrate."

Pamela shakes her head. "I don't think she's going to announce that."

I just hope that whatever she says is good.

"Next Friday is going to be a very special day for the third graders at Fern Falls Elementary," says Mrs. Daily. "We're going to have our first annual Career Day."

Mrs. Daily looks at the class like she really likes the idea. "I want each of you to think about what you might like to be when you grow up. Next Friday, you'll come to school dressed up for the career that you chose, and you'll do a short presentation to the class on what you'd like to be and why."

Before Mrs. Daily can say more, everyone starts talking all at once about what they want to be on Career Day.

"I want to be a pro soccer player," Joey blurts out.

"I want to be a dancer," says Arielle.

"Me too," says Danielle.

"I want to be a violinist," says Pamela.

Mrs. Daily smiles. "I'm glad to see you're all so enthusiastic."

I look around the room to see who else looks enthusiastic about Career Day, and just about everybody does. When Mrs. Daily looks at me, I smile, like I'm excited about Career Day too. But it's hard to feel excited when you don't know what you want to be.

Mrs. Daily walks around the classroom and passes out note cards that say *Career Day* on them. "I'd like each of you to put your name and what you'd like to be on these cards. You have until next Monday to decide."

A lot of people start filling out their Career Day cards. I watch while Pamela writes her name and *violinist* on her card.

When Pamela finishes filling out her card, she looks at me. "Mallory, what are you going to be?"

I shrug my shoulders. "Mrs. Daily said we

have until next Monday to decide."

I slip my card into my backpack and take out my math book.

Pamela stops talking about Career Day and takes out her math book too. But at lunch time, career talk starts up again.

"I'm trying to figure out what my costume will be," Pamela says between bites of spaghetti. "I'm definitely going to bring my violin and play something, but I have to decide what to wear."

All the girls at our lunch table have an opinion.

"Wear a black skirt," says April.

"And a white shirt," says Emma.

"And your hair in a bun," says Dawn.

"Do you think that sounds good?" Pamela asks me.

"Sure," I say. I pick at a noodle. I can't believe Pamela is already thinking about what she's going to wear, and I haven't even thought of what I'm going to be.

"So have you guys decided what you want to be yet?" Pamela asks.

"A flight attendant," says April.

"A teacher," says Emma.

"A gymnastics coach," says Dawn.

Everyone looks at me. "Mallory, what are you going to be?" asks Emma.

I take a big bite of spaghetti.

"Mallory, have you decided?" asks April.

Even though Mrs. Daily said we have a week to decide, I feel like I have to say something. I take another big bite of spaghetti. "I'm going to be a spaghetti eater," I say.

April, Emma, and Dawn laugh at my joke. But Pamela looks serious. "Mallory, you better start thinking about what you want to be," she says.

The bell rings, and for once I'm glad when lunch is over. I don't want to keep talking about Career Day, and I don't have to for the rest of the afternoon.

But on the way home from school, Joey brings it up again. "Hey Mal, what are you going to be on Career Day?"

I groan. I feel like I'm still in the lunchroom. "I haven't decided," I tell Joey.

"Want some help?" he grins. "I can help you think of your career."

"No thanks. I'll think of my own career."

"OK," says Joey, like he'd rather talk about his career than mine anyway. "Do you think Mrs. Daily will let me demonstrate my soccer skills in the classroom?"

"I don't know," I tell Joey. I don't know why he thinks I would know. I'm not exactly a Career Day expert. I'm probably the only kid in my class who doesn't know what they want to be yet.

When we pass Joey's house, his big sister, Winnie, is getting the mail.

"Hey Winnie, the third-graders are having Career Day, and I'm going to be a soccer player," Joey tells his sister.

Winnie rolls her eyes like she can't understand why anybody would actually want to be a soccer player. "I'm not surprised," she says. Then she looks at me. "What are you going to be?"

"I haven't decided yet," I tell her.

Winnie gives me a *how-could-anybody-not-know-what-they-want-to-be-when-they-grow-up* look.

I try to ignore Winnie, but when she's standing there looking at me like it's totally weird that I don't know what I want to be when I grow up, it's not so easy to do.

"Want to skateboard?" Joey asks me.

"We don't have much homework tonight."

"Not today."

I wave good-bye. I don't have time to skateboard. When I get home, I go straight to my desk.

Maybe Joey doesn't have much homework, but I do. I have to figure out what I'm going to be on Career Day.

I take out the Career Day note card that Mrs. Daily gave us.

"Cheeseburger, what do you think I should be when I grow up?" I ask my cat.

But Cheeseburger isn't much help. She just purrs.

I try thinking about other people I know. Dad owns a paint store. Mom teaches music. I don't want to do either of those things.

I think about other careers. Nurse. Chef. Gardener.

I don't really want to be any of those

What am I going to be?

Nurse? Chef? Gardener?

things either. I don't know why it's easy to think of things you don't want to be and hard to think of things you do want to be.

I rub my head, which always helps me think. But today it doesn't.

I look out the window, clean out my sock drawer, and put my hair in a ponytail. I even do my math homework. But none of it helps me think of what I want to be on

Career Day.

Max sticks his head into my room. "Dinner in thirty minutes," he says.

I look at my watch. I can't believe I've been thinking all afternoon and I still haven't thought of anything.

When I go into the kitchen, I smell tacos.

"Mexican night," says Mom.

I sit down in my chair and reach for a taco shell.

"Why the long face?" Dad asks looking at me.

"Mrs. Daily announced today that next Friday is Career Day," I tell him.

"I heard her talking about it in the teachers' lounge," says Mom. "It sounds like fun."

"Fun if you know what you want to be," I say. "But the problem is, I don't."

Dad puts some rice and beans on his

plate. "I'm sure you'll think of something."
Then he smiles. "I have an announcement,"
he says.

I frown. I already heard one
announcement today, and it didn't turn out
to be so great. I hope this one is better.

Dad looks at me. "I think you're going to
like what I have to say. Mom spoke to
Colleen this afternoon. She and Mary Ann
are going to come to visit this weekend."

Max groans. I know he doesn't want to
spend the weekend with Mary Ann, but I
do. I jump up and hug Dad. "Wow! Mary
Ann will be here in four days. That's great
news!" I say to Dad.

Now that Mary Ann's mom and Joey's
dad are married, she and her mom come to
Fern Falls a lot. I still can't believe she's
moving here when the school year is over.

"I better start thinking about what Mary

Ann and I are going to do this weekend," I say to Mom.

Mom laughs. "I'm sure you'll think of something."

I gulp down the rest of my taco, then stand up from the table and dump my plate in the sink. I have some big decisions to make . . . like what I'm going to be on Career Day and what I'm going to do when my best friend gets here.

And I don't have much time to think about either one of those things.

A BAD WEEK

When Dad announced on Monday night that Mary Ann was coming on Friday, I was really happy because I thought I'd only have to wait four days for my best friend to get here. What I didn't know is that those four days would feel like four years.

All week long, it seemed like there was only one thing that anybody talked about, and that one thing was Career Day. And to be honest, it wasn't something I enjoyed talking about. Here's what the rest of the week was like for me:

TUESDAY

On Tuesday, there was only one question that anybody asked me and that one question was not: *Mallory, what kind of sandwich did you bring in your lunch?*

That one question was: *Mallory, what are you going to be on Career Day?*

Pamela asked it. Joey asked it. Arielle and Danielle asked it. And so did just about everybody else in my class.

When I said I didn't know, Arielle and Danielle said it is easy to figure it out. They said all you have to do is decide what you're good at and then be that thing.

Arielle gave me some examples. She said, "Danielle and I are good at dancing, so we're going to be dancers. Joey is good at playing soccer, so he's going to be a soccer player. Pamela is good at playing the violin, so she's going to be a violinist."

When I told Arielle I didn't need any examples, she said it seemed like I did, otherwise, I would know what I wanted to be.

WEDNESDAY

Wednesday was pretty much the same as Tuesday except for one thing . . . it was a whole lot worse!

Talk about Career Day started before I even got to school.

When I was brushing my teeth, Max asked me if I had decided what I wanted to be yet. And on the way to school, Winnie wanted to know too.

When I got to school, I was hoping the thing that people would NOT be talking about was Career Day, but it was exactly what people WERE talking about.

At recess, everybody was talking about what they were going to wear.

"I'm going to wear a navy skirt and top and carry a tray of sodas so I'll look like a flight attendant," said April.

"I'm going to see if Mrs. Daily will let me borrow some of her clothes so I'll look like a

teacher," said Emma.

"I'm going to wear a sweat suit so I look like a gymnastics coach," said Dawn.

"I'm going to see if my dad will let me borrow the clothes he wears when he operates on people so I'll look like a surgeon," said Hannah.

"Mallory, what are you going to wear?" asked Pamela.

When I said I didn't know what I was going to wear because I didn't know what I was going to be, everybody looked at me like I was a jelly bean on a slice of pizza. I felt like a topping that shouldn't be there.

"You *still* don't know what you're going to be?" asked Arielle.

When I told her that I was trying to choose between several things, she asked me what those things were. I told her that I wasn't ready to reveal that information yet.

But here's what I will reveal: Being asked what I was going to be on Career Day when I hadn't thought of anything to be did not make me feel good. AT ALL!

THURSDAY

On Thursday, I *still* didn't know what I was going to be on Career Day, but I knew how I was going to figure it out. When I got home from school, I went to the wish pond, I closed my eyes, and made a wish. I wished that when I opened my eyes I would know what I wanted to be on Career Day.

But when I opened my eyes, I still didn't know what I was going to be.

That night, Dad said I should make a list of ten careers and that I might find one I want to do.

So I made a list.

10 things I, Mallory McDonald,
DO ↗ want to be on Career Day:
NOT   # 1. Potato Peeler
   # 2. Pool Cleaner
   # 3. Farm Hand
   # 4. Fisherman (I <u>hate</u> worms!)
   # 5. Fire Fighter
   # 6. Textbook Writer (I hate textbooks!)
   # 7. Butcher
   # 8. Bug Catcher
   # 9. Blood Test Giver
(I hate blood <u>and</u> tests!)
   # 10. President of the United States

I came up with a list of ten careers. The
only problem was that I didn't want to do
any of them.

FRIDAY

Today is finally Friday! When I woke up this morning, I still hadn't decided what I want to be on Career Day, so when I got to school, I tried talking to Mrs. Daily.

"Our Career Day cards are due on Monday," I said to her, "and I still haven't chosen a career yet. Deciding what you want to be when you grow up is hard," I told her.

"Mallory, this is not a permanent decision," said Mrs. Daily. "Just choose something that is interesting to you."

I thought about what Arielle said earlier in the week, about choosing something that you're good at. What Arielle said and what Mrs. Daily said were two different things. I guess Mrs. Daily could tell I was confused.

She smiled at me. "You can always

change your mind as you grow," she said.

"I don't know how I can change my mind
when I haven't even made it up yet," I said.

Mrs. Daily laughed. She said not to

worry, that she was sure I would think of something over the weekend.

"I hope you're right," I said to Mrs. Daily.

But as I walked home from school with Joey, I couldn't stop my brain from thinking that Mary Ann will be here soon, and once she gets here, I'm not going to have much time to think about what I'm going to be on Career Day.

The problem is: That's exactly what I need to be thinking about because my Career Day card is due on Monday. And no matter what Mrs. Daily says, that worries me.

WEEKEND WORRIES

"You're here! You're here! You're here!"
I throw my arms around Mary Ann and
we jump around in circles in my driveway
three times, once for every *"You're here!"*

"What a nice greeting," Colleen says
with a smile.

"I bet you're going to give Frank a nice
greeting," I say and make a kissy face.

"Mallory!" Mom says my name like what I said shocked her.

But Colleen doesn't look shocked. She laughs. "As a matter of fact, I am planning to give Frank a very nice greeting," she says.

Mom gives me an *I-don't-approve-of-what-you-just-did-young-lady* look.

Colleen puts one arm around my shoulders and the other one around Mom's.

"Don't worry," she says to Mom like what I said didn't bother her at all. "Be happy!"

Colleen looks so happy, that somehow Mom's disapproving look disappears. She and Colleen walk next door to the Winstons' house.

I think about Colleen telling Mom not to worry. I feel like I'm the one she should have said that to. Even though Mary Ann is here and we're going to have a great weekend, it's a little hard not to worry when I know I have to turn in my Career Day card on Monday, and I still haven't decided what I want to be.

I also know I can't spend my whole weekend worrying about Monday. I grab Mary Ann's hand and pull her toward my house. "C'mon," I say. The weekend just started, and at least for now, I'm going to try not to think about Career Day and just think about what Mary Ann and I are going to do. "Should we pick out matching outfits for dinner tonight?" I ask Mary Ann.

Mary Ann giggles. "I brought my pink leggings and striped sweater. I also brought the matching striped baseball hat."

"Great!" I say to Mary Ann. That's one of my favorite outfits that we both have.

When we get to my room, I start looking through my top drawer for my pink leggings. Mary Ann plops down on my bed and pulls Cheeseburger into her lap.

"How's school?" she asks.

I ignore Mary Ann's question. Right now, I'm dealing with more important things, like finding my leggings.

Mary Ann points to the bottom drawer. "Check in there."

I do, and I find my pink leggings neatly folded on the top.

"So have you decided what you're going to be on Career Day?" Mary Ann asks.

I put my pink leggings down on top of my dresser and blow a piece of hair out of my eyes.

I can't believe Mary Ann has only been here for five minutes and we're already talking about the one thing I didn't want to talk about. "How do you know about Career Day?" I ask her.

"Joey told me," Mary Ann says. "He said he's going to be a soccer player, and that everybody knows what they're going to be except for you."

I sit down on the floor in front of my dresser. I really didn't want to spend the weekend thinking about Career Day.

"I just can't figure out what I want to be," I tell Mary Ann.

"You could be a hip hop dancer. That's

what I'm going to be when I grow up."

Mary Ann starts telling me how we can wear matching hip hop outfits, but I interrupt her. "That doesn't sound like something grown-ups can be."

Mary Ann laughs. "Then I'll teach hip hop. My hip hop teacher is a grown-up."

I shake my head *no.* "I don't want to be either of those things," I tell Mary Ann.

"How about a model or a movie star," she says. "That would be fun."

Model?

Movie Star?

I shake my head *no* again. Even though being a model or a movie star sounds like fun, I don't feel like a model or a movie star.

I know Mary Ann is trying to be helpful, but she's not. "Let's get ready for dinner," I say in my *I-don't-want-to-talk-about-this-anymore* voice.

Mary Ann shrugs like she was trying to help me, and it doesn't bother her that I didn't want her help.

But I can tell it does. "I'm sorry," I say. "I didn't mean to hurt your feelings. It's just that I really don't want to spend the whole weekend talking about Career Day."

"No problem" says Mary Ann. "We won't talk about it anymore."

And we don't. We don't say another word about Career Day at dinner that night with the Winstons or at bedtime when we have our official pajama party.

When I wake up on Saturday morning, I rub the sleepies out of my eyes and look at the clock. Mary Ann is still asleep. I shake her. "Wake up!" I say. "If we don't hurry, we're going to miss *Fashion Fran*."

Neither of us wants to do that. Mary Ann and I pop out of bed at the same time. We slip our feet into our fuzzy duck slippers and put on our matching striped baseball caps.

"You get the doughnuts and I'll turn on the TV," I tell Mary Ann.

When Mary Ann comes into the family room with the doughnuts, *Fashion Fran* is just starting. Mary Ann plops down on the couch next to me and hands me a doughnut.

"I have all the latest finds to keep you fashionable this spring," Fran says.

Mary Ann and I watch while she models yellow shorts and pink shirts and baby blue dresses.

"Cute, cute, cute!" says Mary Ann.

Even though Mary Ann and I usually agree, this time I'm not so sure I agree with her. "I think those clothes would have been cuter if the shorts were orange and the shirts were green and the dresses were light purple."

"Hmmm." Mary Ann looks at the TV screen like she's trying to imagine the shorts in orange and the shirts in green and the dresses in light purple.

"That's a good idea," she says. "That would be cute."

I take a bite out of my doughnut. I like when Mary Ann likes my ideas.

We watch while Fran pulls a big, floppy hat out of a box. "I even have a matching sun hat," says Fran. She slips the hat on her head and pulls it down over one eye.

"I like the hat," says Mary Ann.

I look at the big hat on Fran's head and think about it for a minute. "I think it would be cuter if she had a matching baseball cap," I say.

Mary Ann nods her head like she agrees totally. "That is such a great idea!" she says. "I can't believe you thought of that."

I smile. It really is fun when your friend thinks you have great ideas.

"That's all for today." Fran winks with her one eye that isn't covered up by her hat. "Don't forget to join us next week when we announce the winner of the *Kids Can Fashion Design Contest*." Fran blows a kiss to the audience and waves good-bye.

"I can't wait to see who wins and what they designed," says Mary Ann.

I pick a sprinkle off of my doughnut. "I wish I'd entered that contest," I say.

Mary Ann takes a bite of a chocolate covered doughnut. "You should have," she says to me. "I bet you would have won."

Mary Ann holds her hand up in front of her mouth like it's a microphone and she's announcing someone famous. "Mallory McDonald, child fashion designer in New York and on TV." She giggles.

I flick my sprinkle at Mary Ann.

"I've got it!" she says.

I look between her fingers. "A sprinkle?"

Mary Ann laughs like she's got something much more exciting than a sprinkle. "No silly, an idea. You can be a fashion designer for Career Day."

I take a deep breath. "I thought we weren't going to talk about Career Day."

But Mary Ann ignores what I thought

and keeps talking. "It's perfect. You'd make a great fashion designer."

I shake my head. "I didn't even enter the contest."

Mary Ann puts her doughnut down. "So what? Who says you have to enter that contest to be a fashion designer?"

I start to say *no*, but Mary Ann stops me.

"Mallory McDonald, you are meant to be a fashion designer."

I didn't want to spend my weekend talking about Career Day, but something about the idea of being a fashion designer feels good. "Maybe you're right," I say to Mary Ann.

She takes her cap off her head and throws it into the air. It lands behind the couch. "Of course, I'm right!" She grins like she's 100% sure that she is.

I throw my arms around my best friend and give her a big hug. "Thanks so, so much," I tell her. "I *am* going to be a fashion designer on Career Day. I don't know why I didn't think of it before, but it's perfect."

Mary Ann grins. "I'm happy I could help."

I grin too. My Career Day worries are officially over.

A LITTLE LIE

"You're going to be a what?!?"

"I'm going to be a fashion designer," I tell Danielle. I take a pencil and my Career Day card out of my backpack. I start to fill in the blanks on the card.

But Danielle reaches from her desk to my desk and puts her hand on top of my card to stop me before I write too much. "You're going to be a fashion designer?" She says it like she can't believe that's what I'm going to be.

I ignore Danielle and keep filling out my card.

Danielle leans across her desk to talk to her desk mate, Arielle. "Mallory is going to be a fashion designer on Career Day."

"She's going to be a fashion designer?" Arielle repeats what Danielle said, and then she sticks her finger in her ear like it's possible that she's hearing things.

Danielle nods. "It's true!"

"What makes her think she'd be a good fashion designer?" Arielle asks.

Danielle rolls her eyes. "I have no idea."

I know Danielle and Arielle are pretending like I can't hear them talking, but I can, and I don't like what they're saying. I look down at my purple plaid pants and matching poncho. I think I always look fashionable and would make a great fashion designer.

Arielle leans across her desk and whispers something in Danielle's ear. They both start laughing like someone just told them a funny joke.

I try to ignore them and finish filling out my Career Day card, but it isn't easy to ignore people when they're laughing, and you know the thing they're laughing at is you.

Mrs. Daily taps on her desk frog, Chester,

which is what she does when she wants the class to be quiet. "Settle down, girls," she says, looking at Arielle and Danielle.

"Sorry," Danielle says to Mrs. Daily. "We didn't mean to do anything wrong."

"Thank you," Mrs. Daily smiles. She gives them an *I-know-you-didn't-mean-to-do-anything-wrong* look.

But here's what Mrs. Daily doesn't know: Right now while she's smiling at them, they're doing something wrong. Laughing at someone's career choice is wrong. *W-R-O-N-G.* It makes people feel bad. *B-A-D.* Which is exactly how I'm feeling right now.

"Class, please get out your Career Day cards. I'm going to come around and pick them up," says Mrs. Daily.

I hold my card face down. When Mrs. Daily passes my desk, I give it to her.

She turns it over and reads what I've written. "What an interesting choice," she says, and then she smiles at me.

I try to smile back, but I'm not sure what Mrs. Daily meant when she said, *"What an interesting choice."* Maybe she thinks me being a fashion designer is just as silly as Arielle and Danielle think it is.

When Mary Ann told me she thought I should be a fashion designer, it seemed like a good idea. Now I'm not so sure.

Mrs. Daily finishes collecting all of the cards and then tells us to open our Social Studies books.

I'm one of the first ones in the class to open mine.

I'm very happy to stop talking about Career Day and start talking about the American Revolution.

I try to listen while Mrs. Daily tells us

about Betsy Ross, who sewed the first American flag, but it's hard to think about something that happened over two hundred years ago when I can't quit thinking about what happened this morning.

The more I think about Arielle and Danielle laughing at me, the worse I feel.

I wish Mary Ann were here to tell Arielle and Danielle that I would make a great fashion designer.

I watch the clock all morning. When the bell for recess finally rings, I feel like I've been sitting in my seat forever.

"C'mon," Pamela says as everyone is leaving the classroom. "Let's get to the monkey bars before anyone else does."

We run to the monkey bars, but right when we get there, Arielle and Danielle get there too.

"Want to climb to the top?" I ask Pamela. I pretend like I don't even see Arielle and Danielle. Recess is only fifteen minutes and I don't want to spend my favorite fifteen minutes of the day talking to people who laugh at me.

But before we can start climbing, Arielle starts talking. "So Pamela, did Mallory tell you she's going to be a fashion designer on Career Day?"

"Actually, she didn't." Pamela gives me a *how-come-she-knows-more-than-I-do-and-I'm-your-desk-mate* look.

"I was going to tell you," I say to Pamela.

I pretend like I'm at the wish pond and make a wish. *I wish I could explain to Pamela right this very second that I wanted to tell her first thing this morning.* But when Arielle and Danielle found out, they started laughing, and after that, I didn't really want to tell anybody. But I know I can't explain anything to Pamela with Arielle and Danielle standing right here with us.

Arielle gives Pamela a *now-that-I-told-you-something-that-Mallory-didn't-we're-better-friends-than-you-two-are* look. "When I heard that Mallory wanted to be a fashion designer, I was really surprised," she says.

I cross my arms across my chest. "I don't know what the big deal is."

"It's not a big deal." Danielle looks at Arielle like they never said it was a big deal. Then they both look at me like I'm the only one who is making it a big deal.

"It's just that we've never heard you say you were interested in that sort of thing," says Arielle. She looks at Pamela. "You and Mallory are desk mates. She must have told you that she wanted to be a fashion designer."

Pamela shakes her head. "No," says Pamela. "She never told me." Pamela gives me an *I'm-not-sure-I-know-you-as-well-as-I-thought-I-did* look. "We're not saying there's anything wrong with being a fashion designer," explains Danielle. "It's just kind of weird because most people are picking things that they're good at. Arielle and I are going to be dancers. Pamela is going to be a violinist."

"Danielle and I don't even have to find costumes because we can wear what we're going to wear to our recital," says Arielle.

"Do you understand what we mean?" Danielle looks at me like she's a teacher and I'm a student and I might not be getting what she's saying. "We just want to know why you think you'd be a good fashion designer."

I think about how mad I felt this morning when Danielle and Arielle were laughing at me. I feel the same mad feeling coming back, only this time, it's worse.

Danielle and Arielle both give me a *we're-waiting-for-an-answer* look.

I think about what Mrs. Daily said about just choosing something that's interesting to me. But Arielle and Danielle are making me feel like choosing something just because it's interesting isn't a good enough reason to choose it.

Danielle taps her foot on the ground.

I look down at the ground. I know

Danielle is getting sick of waiting, but I'm getting sick of watching Danielle tap her foot. I take a deep breath. "I can explain why I'd be a good fashion designer."

"Well, go ahead," says Arielle.

Pamela looks confused.

I look around the playground. "It's kind of a secret," I say quietly.

Danielle and Arielle lean in. Pamela looks like she's excited to hear what I have to say too. And before I can stop myself, I tell them exactly why I'm qualified to be a fashion designer on Career Day.

THE LIE GROWS

"Mallory, I can't believe you never told me you won the *Fashion Fran Kids Can Design Contest*," Pamela says to me as we walk back to class. "That's so exciting!"

"Yeah," I tell her. It is exciting . . . for whoever really won the contest. I can't believe I said I did. I didn't mean to. It just sort of popped out before I could stop it.

Danielle walks up on one side of me and Arielle on the other. "Excuse us," Arielle says to Pamela. She and Danielle link their arms through mine, like we're all three best friends.

"That is so cool that you won the contest," says Arielle.

"Yeah." I try to smile. But it's hard to look happy about a contest you didn't actually win. I wish I could take back what I said. Hopefully, Pamela, Arielle, and Danielle will forget I even said it.

But they don't seem like they've forgotten anything.

"Tell us all about it," says Pamela.

"Do you win anything?" Danielle asks.

"Are you going to be on TV?" asks Arielle.

I try to swallow, but it feels like there's a TV stuck in my throat. When I said I won the contest, I hadn't thought about what it meant. I didn't think anybody would be asking me a bunch of questions about it.

I try to remember exactly what Fran said the winner of the contest gets. But it's hard to *"remember exactly"* with Danielle and Arielle on both sides of me. I shrug my shoulders. "It's really not such a big deal."

I don't want anyone making this a bigger deal than it really is.

"Mallory, it's a HUGE deal," says Danielle as we walk back into the classroom. She pulls on my arm. "C'mon, we want to know what you won."

"Fashion Fran said the winner of the

contest gets to go to New York, appear on her show, and model the outfit they designed," I say.

I take a deep breath. Fashion Fran did say all that stuff. The only problem is . . . I'm not the one who won it.

"I don't know anyone else who has ever won a contest like that," says Arielle.

"A contest? Did someone win a contest?" Joey walks up beside us.

NO! The last thing I want is for more people to know about this, especially Joey.

I try to send a message from my brain to Danielle's and Arielle's and Pamela's brains that I don't want them to say one thing to Joey about the contest that I did NOT win. But not one of them gets the message.

"I can't believe Mallory didn't tell you!" says Danielle.

"It's so exciting," says Arielle.

"Mallory, why didn't you tell Joey about winning the contest?" Pamela asks me.

"Will someone please tell me what contest you're talking about?" says Joey.

Before I can say a word, Pamela blurts out everything about me winning the contest, going to New York, and being on TV.

"*WOW!*" says Joey. "I can't believe you won!" Joey practically screams when he says it, and when he does, April and Emma come over to where we're standing.

"Who won what?" asks Emma.

"Mallory won a fashion design contest," says Joey.

"Not the *Fashion Fran Kids Can Design Contest?*" asks April.

"That one," says Pamela.

"*COOL!*" screams Emma. "I love *Fashion Fran.*"

"Me too!" screams April like she can't believe she's standing in the same classroom as the person who won that contest. "I entered that contest too." She pulls a piece of paper out of her back pocket with a picture of a girl in jeans, a sweater, and a hat. "This is my design. What did you design?" she asks me.

I clear my throat. It doesn't take me long to think about what I designed, because I didn't design anything. Everyone is looking at me, like they're waiting to hear what I came up with.

I try to think fast. "I, um . . ."

April smiles at me. "I get it," she says. "You don't want to say anything because you want everyone to be surprised when they see your design on TV."

"That's sort of it," I mumble to April. When I speak, my mouth feels fuzzy.

"Tell us more," says Emma.

She starts jumping around and hugging me like nothing could be more exciting or important than hearing every single detail about me winning the contest.

"What do you want to know?" I ask softly.

"*EVERYTHING!*" screams Emma. "What

are you going to do when you go to New York? Do you get to go to the Empire State Building? Do you get to meet the President?" Emma pauses, like she's thinking. Then she starts screaming again. "Oh, who cares about the silly President, you get to meet Fashion Fran!"

"Who gets to meet Fashion Fran?" Hannah comes over, and so does Grace, and Brittany and Dawn, and before I can do anything about it, almost everyone in my class is standing around me while Pamela tells them about the contest.

I feel hot. I pretend like I'm at the wish pond. *I wish I could take back every single thing I said about winning the Fashion Fran Kids Can Design Contest.*

But I can't take anything back with everybody crowding around me. When I said I won this contest, I didn't think it would be such a big deal. I just said it so Arielle and Danielle would think that I'd make a good fashion designer. I didn't think the whole class would be interested.

"Hey, Mallory," says Emma. "Isn't Fran announcing the winner of the contest on her show this Saturday?"

I nod that she is.

Emma puts her lips together and scratches her head. "If she's announcing it on Saturday, how do you already know that you won?"

Everyone gets quiet. It's a good question, and I know they're waiting for my answer.

I look down at my feet. I feel like there are two sides of me right now.

One side wants to tell the truth. I want to say I didn't really win. But the other side feels like I can't do that, now that everybody thinks I won.

I try to think about my two sides and what I should say, but before my brain has a chance to do much thinking, my mouth starts talking. "Fran called my house last night and told me."

Fran called my house last night and told me. I can't believe what I just said.

And no one else can either. Everyone around me starts screaming and jumping like they're at a concert, not in a classroom.

"I can't believe Fran called your house!" screams Dawn. "Tell us everything!"

But before I can say anything, Mrs. Daily walks over. "What's all the excitement about?" she asks.

"Wait till you hear what Mallory won!" says Pamela.

NO! I don't want Mrs. Daily to know anything about this. The first thing she'll do is go straight to the teachers' lounge

and say something to my mom.

But before I can stop Pamela, the whole story about Fran calling my house and me winning the contest and going to New York and being on TV and modeling my design pops out of her mouth.

"Wow," says Mrs. Daily when Pamela is done talking. Then she gives me an *I'm-so-proud-of-you* look. "Mallory, I had no idea you were so talented." Mrs. Daily puts an arm around my shoulder, and then she says the five scariest words I've ever heard: *This calls for a celebration!*

A CELEBRATION

If you ask anybody in my class, they'll tell you when Mrs. Daily brings in doughnuts and hot chocolate on a Tuesday morning, it's a reason to celebrate. But this Tuesday morning, I officially disagree.

"Mallory, aren't you excited about your celebration?" Pamela asks me.

I adjust the hat Mrs. Daily plopped on my head when I walked in the door. Ever since yesterday when Mrs. Daily said, "*This*

calls for a celebration!" I haven't been in a celebratory mood.

I tossed and turned all night just thinking about what Mrs. Daily planned for this morning. And now, looking at the doughnuts and hot chocolate that she brought to class, and the *Congratulations, Mallory!* banner that she hung across the bulletin board, I feel even worse.

Mrs. Daily taps on Chester and asks everyone to settle down. "Before the party starts, there's something I'd like to say." Mrs. Daily smiles at me. "Mallory, will you please come to the front of the room."

I feel like someone super-glued me to my seat.

"Get up!" Pamela grins at me.

Slowly, I stand up, but I can hardly feel my feet move as I walk to where Mrs. Daily is standing. I know I don't deserve to hear whatever she's about to say.

Mrs. Daily puts her arm around me and smiles. "Congratulations on winning the fashion design contest. We're all so proud and can't wait to see you on TV."

Everyone starts clapping and cheering. Some of the boys put their fingers in their mouths and whistle through their teeth.

"Thanks," I mumble. I start to go back to my seat, but Mrs. Daily stops me.

"I'm not through," she says. "I also want to say to the class that I feel you've set a fine example for all of us. There was something you wanted to do and you did it. You didn't just think about it. You did it, and you did it well."

Mrs. Daily looks down at me like she's a mama bird and I'm a baby bird who just learned to fly. "Mallory, I'm very proud of you," says Mrs. Daily. "None of us can

know what we're capable of unless we try. What you did is very special, and I hope you're feeling special right now."

I look down at my shoes and think about what I *really* did.

I am feeling special right now. Especially awful! I'm standing up in front of my class while Mrs. Daily is saying how special I am for something I didn't even do.

Mrs. Daily holds a box of doughnuts out in front of me. "Mallory, since you've given us such a wonderful reason to celebrate, you get to pick the first doughnut."

I look down in the box. There are chocolate covered doughnuts, sprinkle covered doughnuts, glazed doughnuts, and cream filled doughnuts. Doughnuts are one of my favorite foods, but this morning, I don't feel like I deserve any.

"Go ahead," says Mrs. Daily. "It's time to

get the party started."

I pick a plain doughnut. Even though I only take a tiny nibble, I feel like I just swallowed the whole box.

Mrs. Daily sticks a cup of hot chocolate in my hand. "Doughnuts and hot chocolate for everyone!" she says.

When she says that, everyone rushes up to the front of the room and starts picking out doughnuts and taking cups of hot chocolate.

"Mallory, it's so cool we get to have doughnuts and hot chocolate because of you," says Joey.

"I still can't believe you won the contest," says April.

"I can't believe my desk mate is going to be on television!" says Pamela.

What I can't believe is that I haven't passed out. I feel my head to see if I have a fever. I feel so awful, I know I must have some strange disease.

The only reason I ever said that I won the contest was so Danielle and Arielle would stop saying they couldn't understand why I decided to be a fashion designer on Career Day. I didn't think they would tell anybody else. I didn't think that everybody would be making a big deal about it. And I really didn't think my teacher would be throwing a party for me for a contest I didn't even win.

I look down at the marshmallows floating on the top of my hot chocolate. It seems like yesterday was a year ago. So much has happened since I wrote the words *Fashion Designer* on my Career Day card. I wish I could go back in time and write something else, anything other than *Fashion Designer* on that card.

I think about telling everybody the truth . . . right now.

Yesterday, when Pamela told everybody I won the contest, I wanted to say that I hadn't really won. Yesterday, it seemed like it would be hard to tell the truth. Today, it seems like it would be impossible.

I don't know how I can tell the truth when everybody is eating doughnuts and drinking hot chocolate because of me.

I look at the banner hanging on the bulletin board. I wish I could turn myself into a marshmallow and melt away in my hot chocolate.

But when lunchtime comes, I'm still me, sitting at the lunch table like I always do, and everyone around me is still talking about the one thing I don't want to talk about . . . me winning the contest.

"Mallory, when are you going to New York?" Arielle and Danielle ask.

"Mallory, do you get to stay at a fancy hotel?" April wants to know.

"Mallory, what are you going to wear when you meet Fashion Fran?" asks Emma.

Arielle, Danielle, April, and Emma all lean across the table like they can't wait to hear the answers to their questions.

I take a bite of my sandwich. If I answer their questions honestly, I'll be telling more lies. If I tell the truth, they'll know I lied. I don't know which is worse.

The only thing I do know is that I can't wait for lunch to be over. But when it finally is, things don't get much better.

"Class," says Mrs. Daily. "May I have your attention please?" She taps on

Chester. "In honor of Mallory's upcoming trip to New York City, we're going to take a little break from math, and talk about some of the exciting things that Mallory might see when she goes to New York."

Lots of *yeahs* and *awesomes* fill the room. Everyone looks happy that we don't have to do math. Evan and Joey give me a thumbs-up sign.

"Who here has heard of the Empire State Building?" Mrs. Daily asks the class.

Lots of hands go up. Arielle leans over towards my desk. "I'd much rather talk about the Empire State Building than fractions," she whispers.

"Me too," whispers Danielle. She gives me a *you-saved-the-day* smile.

I try to smile back, like I'm glad I saved the day, but the truth is, I know I didn't. Not really.

Pamela slides a note across her desk to me. She smiles as I unfold the square of paper to read what she wrote.

Dear Mallory,
I'm so glad you're my desk mate!
It is so cool that you're going to New York!
When you're on TV will you mention me?
Please say yes!
If the answer is yes, just nod.
You are sooooo cool!
Pamela

When I finish reading the note, I try to swallow, but I can't. Yesterday, when I told a little lie, I never meant for it to grow so big.

It's bad enough that everybody thinks I won a contest that I didn't even enter and that my teacher gave a party to celebrate something I didn't really do. But now, my desk mate wants me to mention her name on a TV show that I'm not going to be on.

Part of me wants to tell her the truth . . . about everything. But Pamela looks so excited about the idea of just having her name mentioned on TV. I know she's waiting for me to nod my head. So I do the only thing I feel like I can do.

I nod.

A PHONE CALL

Sometimes the walk home from school feels like it's taking a long time. This afternoon, it feels like it's taking forever. I just want to get home.

Joey pulls on one of my backpack straps. "Earth to Mallory. For a girl who won a contest, had her own doughnut and hot chocolate party at school, and gets to go to New York and be on TV, you don't look very happy."

I try to smile. "I'm tired," I tell Joey.

He looks at me like he's a doctor and I'm his patient. "You don't look tired."

I am tired. Tired of talking to everybody. All I want to do is curl up on my bed with Cheeseburger.

When I walk inside my house, I head straight to my room, but Mom stops me.

"Hi, Sweet Potato." She gives me a hug. "Good day at school?"

I shrug my shoulders. I really don't want to talk to Mom about my day, but she's in a talkative mood.

"Did I miss anything exciting at Fern Falls Elementary on my day off?" she asks.

I'm not quite sure how to answer that. Some exciting things *did* happen. The problem is . . . I don't think Mom would think they were "exciting" in the way she means. I don't want to tell her what happened.

"Not really." I shake my head. "I'm going to go to my room," I say.

Mom smiles. "Good girl. Starting your homework early. That's what I like to see." She rumples my hair like she approves of my behavior.

But if she knew how I behaved today, I know she wouldn't approve.

I try to smile back and give her a *starting-my-homework-was-exactly-what-I-*

was-planning-to-do look. But I'm not starting my homework unless lying on my bed and adding up all the lies I told today counts as doing math.

I go into my room, lay down on my bed with Cheeseburger, and press my head against my pillow. My brain is so filled up with questions, it hurts.

What if everyone finds out that I didn't really win the contest? What if they're all so mad they never speak to me again? What if Mrs. Daily is so mad she won't even let me stay in her classroom? What if I have to go to a new school because nobody wants me to stay at Fern Falls Elementary?

I look down at Cheeseburger. *What if my own cat finds out what I did and decides to find a new girl to take care of her?*

I feel like crying, but there aren't any tears in my eyes. My stomach hurts.

I need a plan to get myself out of the mess I got into.

I get up, go to my desk, and take out a sheet of paper. I write *Mallory's Plan* across the top.

I rub the sides of my head to help me think. I wait for a good plan to pop into my head. I know there has to be one. The problem is . . . I can't think of one.

I rub. I wait. Nothing.

I sit at my desk for a long time. Still rubbing. Still waiting. Still nothing. It didn't take long to tell a little lie, so I don't know why it's taking so long to find a way to untell it. But it is.

Max sticks his head in my room. "Time for dinner."

"I'll be there in a minute," I tell him.

"You better hurry," says Max. "We're having fried chicken. If you don't come soon, your drumstick might end up in my stomach."

I get up from my desk. I love drumsticks. But tonight, I wouldn't care if that's where mine ended up. I don't feel like eating anything, even something I love.

When I sit down at the table, Mom puts my plate in front of me. I take a tiny bite of chicken, then push my plate away.

Mom takes a bite of her salad and looks at me. "Mallory, don't you like your dinner?"

"It's fine," I tell Mom.

She gives Dad a funny look. Then she looks at me again. "You didn't have a snack after school, and now you're not eating your dinner. Are you feeling OK?"

I push my drumstick from one side of my plate to the other. "I'm fine."

Dad takes a sip of iced tea. "How was

school today?"

"Fine," I tell Dad.

Dad clears his throat. "Mallory, I've heard three *fines*, but you don't seem fine. Did something happen? Is there anything you'd like to talk about?"

Something did happen, but I don't want to talk about it. "Not really," I tell Dad.

Mom starts to say something, but right when she does, the phone rings.

"I'll get it," says Mom. She walks across the kitchen and picks up the phone on the desk. "Hello," she says into the receiver.

Then she smiles. "Mary Ann, so nice to hear your voice."

I'm so glad it's Mary Ann who's calling. This is one of those times when I need to talk to my best friend. If anybody can help me figure out a way to get out of the mess I got myself into, she can.

I push my chair back from the table and walk across the kitchen to where Mom is standing. "I'll pick up in the family room," I mouth to Mom.

But Mom isn't looking at me. She's too busy listening to whatever Mary Ann has to say. "Really," Mom says into the phone. "I had no idea."

I have no idea what Mom is talking about, but I'm not sure I like it.

"A contest? New York? Doughnuts at school?" Mom looks at me. "Joey told you all about it, and you're wondering why Mallory didn't tell you herself?"

Suddenly, I feel as frozen as a Popsicle. Now, I know exactly what Mom is talking about. I might be the first Popsicle in the history of the world to actually throw up. I feel sick.

"I'm sure you would like to talk to her,"

Mom says into the phone. "But Mallory is going to have to call you back later."

I watch Mom put the receiver back on the phone. She looks at me, and when she does, the expression on her face is serious. "Mallory Louise McDonald, your father and I need to see you in the living room."

"Sure." I nod my head like it's no problem. But when Mom uses words like *"Your father and I need to see you in the living room,"* I know there's a big problem. I gently pick up Cheeseburger and gulp.

Today at school, I didn't think things could get any worse. But they just did. Things just got a whole lot worse.

PARENT PROBLEMS

Max takes my drumstick off my plate as I follow Mom and Dad into the living room. "SOMEONE IS IN BIG TROUBLE," he mouths to me.

For once, I agree with Max. Someone is in trouble and that someone is me.

I barely have time to sit down before Mom starts talking.

"Mallory, I'm not exactly sure what happened at school. Before I jump to any conclusions, I'd like the story from you."

I rub the fur behind Cheeseburger's ear. I can see Max standing at the corner of the kitchen listening to our conversation. This is none of his business, but I know Mom isn't concerned about what Max is doing. "I don't know where to start," I tell her.

Mom crosses her arms across her chest. "Young lady, we'd like the truth."

When I told Arielle and Danielle and Pamela that I won the contest, I didn't think I'd end up having to explain the whole thing to my parents. I wish I could go back to yesterday morning and redo it all, but I know I can't.

I put my arms around Cheeseburger and pull her in tight next to me. I clear my throat, then slowly I start talking.

I tell Mom and Dad about everybody in my class but me being good at something, and knowing exactly what they wanted to be on Career Day.

I tell them about Arielle and Danielle saying that they couldn't understand what made me think I'd be a good fashion designer.

I tell them how I told Arielle and Danielle and Pamela that I won the contest, and that before I could stop them, they told everyone in my class, including Mrs. Daily.

I tell them that Mrs. Daily threw a party for me.

And I tell them how much I wanted to tell everyone the truth, but that I didn't feel like I could after I'd already told a lie.

When I'm done talking, Mom and Dad look at each other. Then they both look at me. Neither one of them looks very happy.

"Your father and I are very disappointed in your behavior," Mom says.

"Honestly, Mallory, we can't understand why you would tell everybody you won a contest that you didn't win," says Dad.

I know Dad is waiting for me to explain why I did what I did. But no matter what I say, I don't think he's going to understand. I look down at Cheeseburger who is curled next to me.

"Mallory, we're waiting," says Dad.

I take a deep breath. "I hadn't planned to say I won any contest, it just popped out," I tell my parents.

Mom looks confused, like that isn't much of an explanation. "Mallory, don't I always tell you that it's important to think before you speak?"

I nod my head *yes*. She does always tell me that.

But Dad doesn't look like a head nod is enough of an explanation. He crosses his arms like he's waiting for me to say more.

I cross my toes. I hope Dad understands what I'm about to say. "When I told Arielle and Danielle that I wanted to be a fashion designer on Career Day, they said that they didn't see how I'd make a good fashion designer if I'd never done any fashion design."

"It was silly of them to say that," says Dad.

I double cross my toes. Maybe Dad does understand. I think back to what happened yesterday on the playground.

"It was silly," I say. "And mean, too. And they kept saying it over and over again, until finally I said I won the contest because I didn't know what else to say."

I stop talking. I think that explanation makes sense, and I hope Dad will too.

He's quiet for a minute. I can tell he's thinking about what I said. "Mallory, the girls had no right to say to you what they did," Dad says.

I uncross my toes. "Exactly!" I spring off

the couch to hug Dad. All my toe crossing paid off. I'm so glad he understands.

But he holds out his hand like he's a traffic patroller and he's telling me to stop. "Young lady, sit down."

I take a deep breath. I know Dad isn't through.

"Even though the girls shouldn't have said what they did, you shouldn't have said what you did either. It was wrong of you to say something that wasn't true," he says.

"I wish I hadn't," I say quietly.

Dad looks me in the eye. "It's worse than that though. After you said it, you let people go on believing it was true. You even let Mrs. Daily throw a party for you."

I take a deep breath. I know Dad won't say a thing until I explain why I did that, and the truth is, there is no good explanation.

"Dad, I wish I hadn't done that either. But once I said it, it was hard to un-say it. If I could take it all back, I would."

"Mallory," Dad says my name in a low, deep voice. "You told a lie."

"I'm really sorry." My voice is so low, I can barely hear myself talk.

Dad kneels down in front of me and tilts my chin up so I'm looking him right in the eye. "We're not the ones you need to apologize to."

"Mallory Louise McDonald." Mom says my name like she's a judge and I'm on trial and about to be sentenced. "What you did was wrong. There is never a good reason to lie. Tomorrow when you go to school, you are going to have to tell Mrs. Daily and your friends the truth about the contest."

I really don't want to do that. As happy as everyone was for me when they thought

I won the contest is as mad as they are going to be when they find out I made the whole thing up. I can feel hot tears starting to form behind my eyes. I reach down to pet Cheeseburger, but when I do, she jumps off of the couch and walks into the kitchen.

"Mom, what am I going to say?" I can't imagine how I'm going to explain to my

SELF-PORTRAIT OF A POOR, SAD GIRL WHO HAS TO TELL HER CLASS THE TRUTH

class that I didn't really win the contest.

"Mallory, you got yourself into this mess, and I expect you to find a way to get out of it," she says.

"Honesty is always the best policy," says Dad. I already know that honesty is the best policy. The problem is that being honest after you've said something that isn't true isn't easy to do. I can feel the tears starting to roll down my cheeks.

I think about what Mom said about me getting myself out of this mess.

There are a lot of things I look forward to, like skateboarding, painting my toenails, and watching TV on Saturday mornings, but there is something I'm not looking forward to, and that's getting myself out of this mess.

I'm not lying when I tell you I'm not looking forward to it one single bit.

THE TALE OF
THE TERRIFYING
TEACHER

Once upon a time, there was a third grade teacher who gave a doughnut and hot chocolate party for a student who she thought was "special."

She made a banner for that "special" girl.

She went on and on and on to the class about how "special" the girl was.

She even cancelled math ... all on account of that "special" girl.

It would be fair to say that on that day, that teacher thought that girl was the best, nicest, most perfect student in the whole, wide world.

But the next day when the girl arrived at school, things took a turn for the worse.

It all started when the girl asked the teacher if she could talk to her privately outside the classroom. The girl explained to the teacher that due to circumstances kind of out of her control, she accidentally told a little lie. She told her what she had done, and then she waited, hoping that the teacher would understand. But sadly for the girl, the teacher did not understand, and that's when terrifying things began to happen.

First, the teacher turned many different colors, including red, purple, green, and blue.

She looked mad. Very, very, very mad.

Next, the teacher spoke to the girl in a low, mean voice. She crossed her arms and tapped her feet, and used harsh words, like lying and deceit.

Then, she did the most terrifying thing of all. She marched the girl back into the classroom and as she did, she uttered the following words:

"You've got some explaining to do, young lady!"

Poor, poor girl.

TELLING
THE TRUTH

Telling the truth after you tell a lie is something that's not fun to tell at all. And that's exactly what Mrs. Daily says I have to tell my whole class.

I don't want to walk back into the classroom and tell the truth.

I'd like to tell Mrs. Daily that I can't because my sneakers are stuck to the floor.

But right now, I don't think telling Mrs. Daily a lie, even a little one about stuck sneakers, is a good idea.

Even though I'm usually a fast walker, I walk as slowly as I possibly can as I follow Mrs. Daily back into the classroom.

"C'mon, Mallory!" Mrs. Daily pulls on my arm like she's trying to speed me up.

When we get inside, I close my eyes and make a quick wish: *I wish I could be anywhere but here right now.* When I reopen my eyes, I'm still right where I was before I made my wish.

"Everyone, please take your seats," says Mrs. Daily.

After everyone does, she gives me a *Mallory-are-you-ready* look.

I'm definitely NOT ready. Even though I wish I had never said that I won the contest, I also wish that I didn't have to do this. Mrs. Daily is the only one who knows the truth yet, but I feel like once I've said what I have to say, there's only one thing that everybody will be thinking about me, and that one thing is: BIG LIAR.

I might as well get a T-shirt that says that on it.

I look across the room at Pamela and Joey. I can only imagine what my best friends will be thinking when they hear what I have to say.

"Class, Mallory has something she'd like to say to you," says Mrs. Daily.

Everybody looks at me like they hope that what I have to say is exciting.

"Is today Show and Tell?" April asks.

"Did Mallory win something else?" Emma wants to know.

"Do we get more doughnuts?" asks Pete.

"No doughnuts today." Mrs. Daily's

mouth is as straight as a ruler. There's no trace of a smile anywhere. "Mallory doesn't have anything to show you, but she has something to tell you."

Mrs. Daily nods her head at me. I know that means she's ready for me to begin.

I see Joey looking at me. I'm sure he thinks I have something good to say. I wish I did. I clear my throat. But no sound comes out.

"Mallory." Mrs. Daily says my name in a quiet, serious way.

I take a deep breath. Even more slowly than I walked into the classroom, I start talking. "I have something to say."

My words feel like they don't want to come out of my mouth. I stop and look down at my sneakers. Then I start again. "I wish I didn't have to say this . . ."

It feels like there's a lump in my throat

and the words are having a hard time getting past it. But I make them come out.

"I said I won the *Fashion Fran Kids Can Design Contest* and that I get to go to New York and be on TV. But the truth is, I didn't really win and I don't get to go to New York or be on TV. I made up the whole thing. I wish I hadn't, but I did and I'm really, really, really sorry."

When I finish talking, everyone is quiet. No one seems like they know what to say. I cross my toes and make a wish. *I wish my class will understand and not be mad that I lied to them.*

I wait for someone, anyone, to say something, like: *Mallory, we understand. Everyone makes mistakes. No big deal.*

But no one says a thing. My classroom has never been this quiet.

Mrs. Daily breaks the silence. "Thank

you, Mallory," she says. She looks at the class. "It's never easy to admit when you did something wrong."

She walks over to where I'm standing. I've never felt so small and Mrs. Daily has never seemed so big. "You may sit down," she says like we're through with this subject.

Maybe Mrs. Daily is through, but when I get back to my seat, other people still have questions. "Mallory, you didn't win the contest?" April looks confused.

"You don't get to go to New York or be on television?" asks Dawn.

"Why did you say you won if you didn't?" asks Pete.

"It was a dumb thing to say, and if I'd thought about it before I said it, I wouldn't have . . ." I start to say "said it," but Mrs. Daily stops me.

"Class, it's time for math," she says.

"Please open your workbooks to page 57."

For once, I'm glad it's time for math.

I reach into my desk to get out my workbook. But when I do, I can't help looking at Arielle and Danielle. They're whispering to each other, and looking at me with *we-can't-believe-you'd-lie-about-winning-a-contest* looks on their faces.

Pamela is looking at me in a funny way too. I know Pamela, and I know there's no way she will understand why I would say something like that if it wasn't true.

Then I look across the classroom at Joey, and as soon as I do, I wish I hadn't. He has a look on his face that is much worse than Arielle's and Danielle's or Pamela's. He looks disappointed.

I try to smile at Joey. A teeny, tiny, *I'm-sorry* smile. But he doesn't smile back.

I feel even worse now than I did when I

was telling the class that I lied about the contest. I can't stand thinking about Joey being disappointed in me.

And I know he is because he doesn't say anything to me all morning or at lunch. And he isn't the only one. When I sit down at lunch, all of the girls who I always sit with and who always talk to me, treat me like I'm not even there.

"Who wants part of my peanut butter and marshmallow sandwich?" Danielle asks.

Even though Danielle knows that that is

my favorite kind of sandwich, she leans across me and gives one square of her sandwich to Pamela and another one to April.

"Who wants one of my Oreos?" Arielle asks. She gives everyone at the table a cookie . . . everyone except me.

She and everyone else at the table pull their cookies apart at the same time, while I just sit there. I know everyone is mad at me because I told a lie. But everyone seems to only be remembering that I lied and forgetting that I also apologized.

The afternoon passes by so slowly. Every time I look at Pamela, she looks down at the books on her desk, like she's really concentrating on her schoolwork. But I know what she's really concentrating on is avoiding me.

When the bell finally rings at the end of

the day, I grab my backpack and race out the door. Usually, Joey waits for me. But today, he doesn't.

I have to run to catch up with him. "Hey, do you want to skateboard when we get home?" I ask him.

Joey loves to skateboard, but he doesn't say he wants to.

I try again. "We can teach Cheeseburger some new cat tricks," I say.

But Joey doesn't say that he wants to do that either. He just keeps walking.

"We can play with Murphy," I say. I know how much Joey likes playing with his dog. But he doesn't even say he wants to play with his dog.

Joey doesn't say anything to me.

I walk in front of him and hold out my hand to stop him like we're playing Red Light, Green Light and he just got a red

light. "I know you're mad at me." I try to stop him, but he keeps walking until he gets to his house. He walks inside without even saying good-bye.

Joey has never done that.

My parents are mad at me. My teacher is mad at me. My friends at school are mad at me. And now, Joey is mad at me.

Just when I thought things couldn't get any worse, they do.

Things just keep getting worse and worse and worse.

FACING THE TRUTH

When I get home, I go straight to my room, shut my door, and cover my head with my pillow. I don't want to talk to anybody at my house. Not Mom. Not Dad. Not Max.

The only person I want to talk to lives next door and he's not talking to me. I take the pillow off my head. "I have to do something," I say to Cheeseburger.

She rolls over on my bed and purrs. I think it's a *then-go-do-it* purr.

I look at Cheeseburger. "You're right. I'll be back," I tell my cat.

I walk next door to Joey's house and ring his doorbell.

Winnie answers the door. "Someone is in the doghouse, and I'm not talking about Murphy," she says when she sees me. "Joey told me what you did, and I can't believe it!" She grins like she's enjoying making me feel worse than I already do.

"May I come in and see Joey?" I ask.

Winnie stretches her arm across the doorway, like she's blocking me from coming inside. "Um, see, the thing is, I don't actually think Joey will want to see you."

Most days Winnie won't even talk to

Joey, and today, she's acting like his body guard. "Can I at least try?" I ask.

"Joey is pretty mad," says Winnie. "And in case you didn't know this about him, he almost never gets mad at anybody."

I do know this about Joey, and that's why I feel as badly as I do. I can't stand being the one he's mad at. "I have to talk to him," I say ducking under Winnie's arm.

I run down the hall to Joey's room. The

door is open so I walk right in.

Joey is sitting at his desk. When I walk in, he looks at me, but he doesn't say anything.

I start. "Joey, I know you're mad at me. I'm really sorry I told a lie."

Joey twirls around in his desk chair. "I just can't believe you lied about something like that." He shakes his head like no part of him can understand what I did.

"I said I was sorry."

"You told the whole class and you even let Mrs. Daily throw a party for you. I just don't understand why you would do that."

I feel worse now than I did when I had to talk to Mrs. Daily, or last night when I had to talk to Mom and Dad, or today when I had to tell the class that I lied. I feel awful right now because I did something that I know Joey wouldn't have done, and I know he's disappointed that I did it.

I sit down on Joey's bed. I don't know if Joey's going to understand. But I try to explain.

"I said I won the contest because everybody in our class is good at something, and everybody knew right away what they wanted to be on Career Day. When I said I wanted to be a fashion designer, Arielle and Danielle said they didn't see why I thought I would make a good fashion designer."

I can tell by looking at Joey that that doesn't make much sense to him, so I keep explaining.

"I said I won the *Fashion Fran* contest so they would think there was a reason why I would make a good fashion designer."

When I finish talking, Joey looks like he sort of understands.

"I get it," he says. "But you still shouldn't

have lied. Who cares what Arielle and
Danielle think anyway?"

I pretend to look around Joey's room like
I'm looking for someone who cares. "I
don't know. Is there someone here who

cares what they think?"

Joey smiles.

At least he knows I'm trying to make a joke. "Joey, I'm really sorry."

Joey nods like he accepts my apology. Then he gets a serious look on his face. "Mallory, one of the things my mom used to say before she died is that it's a lot easier to tell the truth than it is to face the truth."

I know Joey gets a little sad when he thinks about his mom. I also know his mom was right about what she said.

"It would have been a lot easier to be honest and just say that I wanted to be a fashion designer because I like fashion design than it was to explain why I said I won a contest that I didn't really win," I say.

Joey nods.

"Your mom must have been a very smart lady," I say to Joey.

Joey nods again. "She was."

I smile at Joey. I'm glad I came over and straightened things out with him.

"Maybe tomorrow after school, we can skateboard or teach Cheeseburger some new tricks or play with Murphy if you want to," I say.

Joey grins. "Sounds great!"

I think it does too. And I feel great all the way home.

At least I feel great until I get home. When I walk in the front door, Max pops off the couch. He has a piece of paper in his hands. "I have a message for you," he says.

Whatever the message is, Max looks excited to deliver it.

"It's from Birdbrain," he says. "She called and wanted me to write this out for you."

I take the note from Max and read it.

Mallory,
WHY DIDN'T YOU TELL ME YOU
WON THE FASHION FRAN
KIDS CAN DESIGN CONTEST?
We are best friends, and best
friends are supposed to tell each
other everything. Especially
stuff like that.
From, Mary Ann
(as dictated to Max)

When I'm done reading, I crumple the
note in my hand.

Max grins. "Have fun answering that
one," he says.

I pick up the crumpled note off the floor.

I don't think it's going to be much fun,
but I know I have to answer it.

CAREER DAY

Mom walks into my room. "I found this behind the couch." She puts Mary Ann's striped baseball cap on my dresser. Then she reaches up to turn out my light. "Bedtime," she says.

"I can't go to bed yet!" I take two butterfly clips off the pile on my bed and stick one in the front of my hair and one behind Cheeseburger's left ear.

"Mallory, it's already 15 minutes past

your bedtime," says Mom.

I look at the clock on my nightstand table. "I know," I say. I stick another butterfly clip on the back of my head and one behind Cheeseburger's right ear. "But tomorrow is Career Day. I still haven't written my speech or found a costume."

I don't tell Mom why I haven't written my speech. But the truth is . . . even though I signed up to be a fashion designer, I feel funny about being one after everything that happened. Part of me wishes I could switch to a different career. But part of me just wants to find something to make my presentation extra special.

Mom blows out air like she's getting frustrated. "Sticking clips in your hair and Cheeseburger's fur isn't going to help you come up with something."

I reach up and feel my head, and then I

pet my cat. We're both covered in butterflies. "It might," I tell Mom.

Mom puts her hands on her hips. "Mallory Louise McDonald, you have half an hour, and then it's bedtime."

"Thanks," I say to Mom. But I don't know what I'm thanking her for. I've been thinking all night and I haven't come up with anything yet. I will never write a speech and find a costume in 30 minutes.

I walk into my bathroom with Cheeseburger, and I hold her up so we're both looking in the mirror. "Don't we look cute with matching hairstyles?" I say to her.

Cheeseburger doesn't look like she really thinks so, but I do.

I don't know why I didn't think of it before. I put Cheeseburger down and go straight to my desk. I start writing my speech. Then I take construction paper out of my bottom drawer. I cut and write and paste until I've done what I need to do.

When I'm done, I look in my closet and in my bottom drawer to get out the other things I need. I put everything in a bag and write *Career Day* on the outside.

I put on my pajamas and brush my teeth. "Good night," I yell up to Mom and Dad.

"Good night," Mom calls down the stairs. "Are you ready for Career Day?"

"I'm ready," I tell Mom. Then I cross my toes. I just hope when morning gets here, Mom will go along with my plan.

When morning arrives, I put on my pink leggings with the matching striped sweater and baseball cap. Then, I grab my *Career Day* bag and Cheeseburger.

"Good morning," I say to Mom and Dad and Max when I walk into the kitchen.

Mom gives me a funny look. "Mallory, aren't you supposed to be wearing your costume for Career Day?"

"I'm wearing part of my costume." Then I hold up my bag and my cat. "And I'm bringing part of my costume."

Mom looks confused. "Mallory, is Cheeseburger part of your costume?"

I nod my head.

Max takes my baseball cap off my head. "Did you lose your brain? You know you can't take your cat to school."

I ignore Max. I show Mom what's in my bag. I explain why I have to take Cheeseburger to school.

I cross my toes extra-hard that Mom won't say *no*, and this time it works.

Mom smiles like she approves of my plan for Career Day. "I don't see why

Cheeseburger can't go to your classroom for a little while. When you're done with your presentation, bring her to me and I'll keep her in the music room. Let me call Mrs. Daily to make sure she won't mind."

I wait while Mom dials her number. I listen while she explains what I want to do. Then I smile when Mom hangs up the phone and says Mrs. Daily agreed to it.

I put my bag down and give Mom a huge hug. "Thanks!" I tell her. I grab a granola bar, my bag, and my cat as I walk out the door. I hope everyone likes my Career Day presentation.

When I get to school with Cheeseburger, everyone is wearing their costumes.

Joey has on his soccer clothes. Pete is dressed like a basketball player. Pamela has on a long blue skirt and a white blouse, and she's carrying her violin. Arielle and

Danielle are dressed like they just came from their dance recital.

"I like your costume," I say to Dawn. She looks like a gymnastics coach.

"Thanks!" She blows the whistle that's hanging around her neck. "You can't bring your cat to school. It's Career Day, not Pet Day."

"It's OK," Mrs. Daily says to Dawn. "I gave Mallory permission."

"I don't get it," says Dawn. "If Mallory is a fashion designer, why does she need to bring her cat to school?"

Mrs. Daily and I look at each other and smile. "You'll find out in a few minutes," she says to Dawn.

Then Mrs. Daily looks around the room admiring all of the costumes. "You all look great," she says. "Now let's get the first Fern Falls Elementary Career Day started!"

Everybody claps and screams like no one can wait to get started.

Mrs. Daily asks for a volunteer to go first. Lots of hands shoot in the air. Mrs. Daily picks Pamela.

Pamela walks to the front of the classroom. She reads her speech and plays a violin solo. "This is the same solo I'll be playing at my recital," she tells the class.

When she finishes, everyone claps.

"That was an excellent speech and you play beautifully," says Mrs. Daily. "I'm sure you will do a wonderful job at your recital."

Pamela sits. Mrs. Daily calls on Pete.

Pete tells everyone he wants to be a basketball player. He demonstrates his dribbling skills. When he does, his ball almost knocks Chester, Mrs. Daily's desk frog, off of her desk.

Mrs. Daily doesn't seem upset. She catches Chester just in time. "Good job, Pete," she says.

He sits down. Then, Mrs. Daily calls on Hannah, then April, then Evan, and then Arielle and Danielle, who go together since they want to be the same thing.

Everyone talks about what they want to be and why. Arielle and Danielle give a dancing demonstration.

"Excellent job!" Mrs. Daily says.

I pet Cheeseburger. I hope Mrs. Daily calls on us soon.

"Joey, your turn," says Mrs. Daily.

Joey walks to the front of the classroom. He gives a great speech about being a professional soccer player, then he kicks the ball up and down the aisles of the classroom, avoiding every desk, chair, and backpack.

"You're very skilled," says Mrs. Daily, who looks relieved when Joey's turn is over.

"Mallory, your turn," she says when Joey is back in his chair.

I walk to the front of the classroom with my bag and my cat.

I wasn't nervous when I wrote my

presentation, but thinking about giving it makes me feel like all of the butterflies that were on top of my head last night are fluttering around in my stomach today.

I clear my throat and begin.

"Good morning fellow classmates. When I grow up, I want to be a fashion designer. I think this is an important job because fashion designers design clothes. Clothes help people have style. And style is one way of showing the world how you are unique. But I don't want to just be a regular fashion designer. I want to be a fashion designer who designs matching outfits for people and their pets. This is also an important job because pets deserve to have a unique style too."

I see Arielle roll her eyes, like she doesn't get why anyone would want to design matching outfits for people and their pets.

I ignore her. "Now I will show you just how cute matching outfits can be." I reach into the bag and pull out Mary Ann's striped baseball cap and put the hat on Cheeseburger's head.

Even though Mary Ann's cap is too big for Cheeseburger, I think she looks cute.

I smile at the class and hold my cat up so they can see that we match.

Everyone claps.

"Thank you, Mallory," says Mrs. Daily. "You may sit down now."

"But I'm not finished yet," I say.

Mrs. Daily looks surprised, but nods, like it's OK for me to continue.

My presentation was easy to give until now. The part that's left is harder. "I want to say that I still feel terrible about what I said to all of you about winning the contest and going to New York."

I reach into my bag and pull out the certificates I made out of construction paper last night. I walk around the classroom and give one to everyone. "This certificate is for one free custom-designed outfit for you and your pet. I'll help you find something that matches, and if you don't have a pet, you can use a stuffed animal."

I end up at Mrs. Daily's desk. I give her a certificate too.

Then I look at my class. "Thank you very much. The end."

"Mallory, a wonderful presentation, creative costume, and very generous offer that I plan to take you up on one day." Mrs. Daily smiles at me. "Excellent job!" she says.

I smile back. "Thanks!" I say to my teacher. That was exactly what I wanted to hear. I walk back to my desk and sit down. When I do, Pamela gives me the thumbs up sign.

I know she liked my presentation, but I still feel like I owe her one more apology about everything that happened. "Pamela, I'm really sorry I lied to you," I whisper.

She looks at me like she understands. "It's OK," she says. "But if you ever get to be on TV, you have to promise to mention me."

I grin and nod my head *yes.*

Career Day turned out to be great. Maybe I will grow up to be a fashion designer who designs matching outfits for people and their pets. Maybe I'll even get to be on TV someday. Or maybe, I'll be something else. Who knows.

The good news is . . . I don't have to decide for a long, long time.

The Daily News

CAREER DAY SPECIAL REPORT
By Pamela Brooks

Career Day was a big hit.

"The presentations were fantastic and so were the costumes," Mrs. Daily said when interviewed.

If you don't believe me, just take a look at this photo.

When Mrs. Daily's third-grade students were asked if they had any advice for future third graders about Career Day, one student, Miss Mallory McDonald (a.k.a. my desk mate) had a lot to say.

"When it comes to choosing a career, pick something that sounds like fun and don't worry about what other people think."

Thanks Miss McDonald! That sounds like good advice.

And thanks to all of the Fern Falls Elementary third-graders for making Career Day a big success!

A LETTER TO MARY ANN

Dear Mary Ann,

The only thing that travels faster than a speeding train is a lie. I'm sorry you had to hear about me winning the contest from Joey.

The truth is, I didn't really win the contest. I just said I did because some of the girls in my class were saying they didn't know why I thought I would be a good fashion designer. I felt like I had to say something. So I said I won.

But then, I had to tell everyone the truth. And that was no fun at all.

So I made up two new rules:

Rule #1: Never say you won a contest when you didn't.

Rule #2: As official LBF's (lifelong best friends), if we ever win anything, we'll tell each other first.

I think those are good rules, don't you?

Also, I thought you might want an official report on Career Day, so here goes.

After everything that happened with the contest, I felt kind of funny being a plain old fashion designer, so I decided to be a fashion designer who designs matching outfits for kids and their pets.

Cheeseburger got to go to school with me since I designed matching outfits for us. We both wore our matching baseball caps. (I hope you don't mind that Cheeseburger borrowed yours.)

We looked cute, cute, cute!

Well, Career Day is over and I'm kind of glad. And there's something else I'm glad about: *Fashion Fran* is starting in five minutes!

Got to go. Got to watch!

Big, huge hugs and kisses!

Mallory

P.S. It's me again (in case you are wondering who added this P.S.). I'm glad I didn't mail this letter before the show, because now I have something important to tell you.

Fashion Fran announced that she's having another fashion design contest this fall! Well, guess who's going to enter it? (If you guessed me, you guessed right.)

The winner gets to go to New York for a weekend. I want to go so badly! I'm crossing my toes now and leaving them crossed until I hear who wins the big trip.

Will you cross your toes for me?

OK. That's it. Now I've really got to go. Got to draw!

P.P.S. What do you think of matching beachwear for girls and their cats?

I just love, love, love it, especially the sunglasses. I hope Fran will too!

Carolrhoda Books
A division of Lerner Publishing Group, Inc.
241 First Avenue North
Minneapolis, MN 55401 U.S.A.

Website address: www.lernerbooks.com

Library of Congress Cataloging-in-Publication Data

Friedman, Laurie B.
        Honestly, Mallory! / by Laurie Friedman ; illustrations by Bárbara Pollak.
           p.   cm.
        Summary: When Mallory cannot decide what to be on Career Day, it makes
    her feel like she is not good at anything and she ends up telling a lie that
    quickly gets out of control.
        ISBN: 978-0-8225-6193-4 (lib. bdg. : alk. paper)
        [1. Honesty—Fiction. 2. Peer Pressure—Fiction. 3. Schools—Fiction.
    4. Occupations—Fiction.] I. Pollak, Barbara, ill. II. Title.
    PZ7.F89773Hon 2007
    [Fic]—dc22   2006101328

Manufactured in the United States of America
4 5 6 7 8 9 — BP — 13 12 11 10 09 08